Ginkgo AND Moon

Lisa Mertins

HOUGHTON MIFFLIN COMPANY

Boston   1996

Dedicated with love to
Joe, Daniel, Jordan, Ethan, and Hannah

For information about this and other Houghton Mifflin trade and reference
books and multimedia products, visit The Bookstore at Houghton Mifflin on
the World Wide Web at http://www.hmco.com/trade/.

Manufactured in the United States of America

Book design by Mina Greenstein
The text of this book is set in 14.5 -point Stempel Schneidler.
The illustrations are alkyd paints on masonite, reproduced in full color.
Photographs of the artwork are by Curt Norris.

HOR 10 9 8 7 6 5 4 3 2 1

Library of Congress Cataloging-in-Publication Data
Mertins, Lisa
Ginkgo and moon / by Lisa Mertins
p. cm.
Summary: a ginkgo tree tries to attract the moon's attention, but
the moon is too busy chasing after the sun to notice the humble ginkgo.
ISBN 0-395-73576-9
[1. Ginkgo—Fiction. 2. Trees—Fiction. 3. Moon—Fiction. 4. Nature—Fiction.
5. Seasons—Fiction.] I. Title PZ7.M54565Gi 1996
[Fic]—dc20 94-40960 CIP AC

GINKGO LOVED MOON. Each night he watched her cross the sky, leaving stars like silver footprints behind her.

He found her luminous round
face beautiful beyond compare—
and his leaves whispered to her.

But Moon didn't notice Ginkgo.

She was busy following Sun,
who was always beyond her reach.
And Ginkgo could not compete with
one so splendid as Sun.

So Ginkgo made a plan. He murmured to the flowers beneath
his shade. Surely their marvelous perfume could reach the heavens.
Would Moon notice Ginkgo then?

That night as Moon slowly approached, the flowers nodded their heads and their scent rose. But as the air thinned at the edge of space, the smell of the flowers faded.

Moon passed by without a glance toward Ginkgo.

Ginkgo's spirit did not dim. He rustled his leaves toward countless summer-bright butterflies.

Ginkgo thought that if they danced above him, they would catch Moon's attention.

The butterflies fluttered as Sun left the sky. But without Sun's light, the wings of the butterflies lost their glory. Moon crossed the sky, still chasing Sun.

Ginkgo's hope faltered as the butterflies slipped away.

Then, one evening, as a mist swirled beneath Ginkgo's branches, he noticed the blinking light of a firefly. Ginkgo's leaves quivered as he urged one firefly after another to cling to him.

Soon each leaf was covered with a shimmering light.

Surely Moon would notice Ginkgo ablaze with the light of a thousand fireflies.

Out of the corner of Moon's eye, she noticed a still light fixed to the earth, one she could gaze at without a chase. Moon considered this wondrous glow.

But as Sun slipped behind the sea, he too noticed the small shining tree. Sun couldn't bear the thought of a light as fine as his own. He called the wind, and it blew toward Ginkgo.

As the wind approached, all of Ginkgo's leaves and clinging fireflies were sent rushing skyward.

Ginkgo was left leafless and alone.

Moon realized when she felt a leaf brush her cheek that jealous Sun had snuffed out the light of the little tree.

"Poor Ginkgo," thought Moon. "He was so fine and golden, and what a show he put on for me."

Ginkgo was bare and humble. All his plans had failed.

For a time, Ginkgo couldn't bear to look at the sky. But when he did, he noticed something strange and different, something that for a moment made him forget his leafless self.

That night and each night following, Moon grew smaller and smaller, until one night, much to Ginkgo's astonishment, Moon disappeared completely.

Winter surrounded Ginkgo and, though Moon returned, Ginkgo
abandoned his lofty plan to gain her affections.

In his position of silent longing, his stark branches reaching in Moon's direction, Ginkgo's heart drifted toward slumber.

When the sounds of living things returned, Ginkgo awoke. His leaves were reappearing, tiny and silken. And soon, their springtime fan-flapping lifted Ginkgo's spirit.

Gentle breezes warmed the sky and throughout the summer
months, Ginkgo watched Moon's many transformations.

On the nights Moon disappeared, Ginkgo thought that Moon and Sun were in some bright place together, laughing and happy.

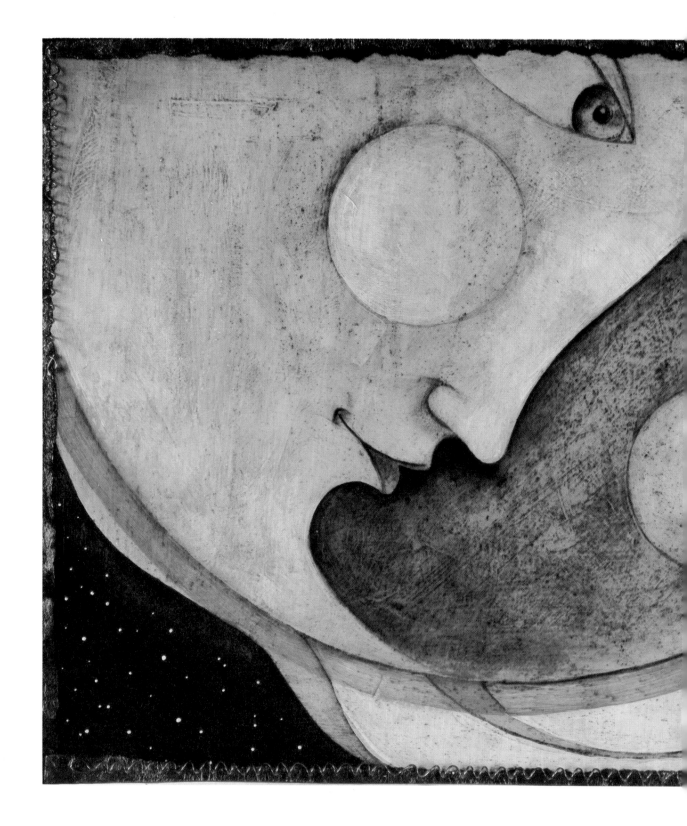

Then, one blustery night, something extraordinary happened. Moon appeared in a glorious way, bigger and brighter than Ginkgo had ever seen her. She paused in the sky, gazing at him so intently that Ginkgo was bathed in a brilliant light.

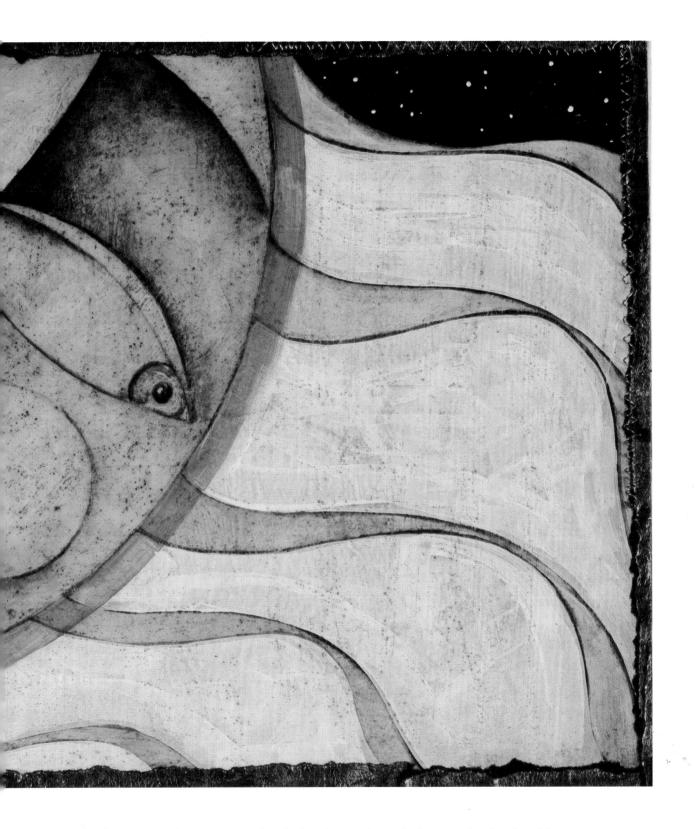

All the time that Moon had thickened and thinned, she had been
saving her light, and now she was pouring it down in a single beam onto
Ginkgo, setting his leaves aglow.

His heart was joyous.
Ginkgo knew without a doubt
that Moon had noticed him,
for all of his leaves were a
grand and radiant yellow.

So now, although Moon never stops her flight across the sky, she is no longer interested in chasing Sun. Moon is forever waxing and waning, saving her light for that certain autumn night when she can pause in the sky to shower Ginkgo with a beam so bright that his leaves turn a magnificent yellow.

And Ginkgo reminds Moon of his love for her by waiting for the strongest, coldest wind so that he can fling his beautiful moon-brightened leaves toward the heavens.